# THE GAMES WE PLAY

# THE GAMES WE PLAY

*Alex Pattillo*

iUniverse, Inc.
New York  Lincoln  Shanghai

# The Games We Play

iUniverse, Inc.

For information address:
iUniverse, Inc.
2021 Pine Lake Road, Suite 100
Lincoln, NE 68512
www.iuniverse.com

The characters and places described in this book are not meant to represent any specific person or place.

ISBN: 0-595-29099-X

Printed in the United States of America

# CHAPTER 1

On a hot summer afternoon in 1967 three boys, all in their tenth year, trampled over palm branches and tree roots in single file through a small area of palms and huge moss covered trees. One of them called out, "Do ya'll know exactly where it is?"

Jonathan, the leader, called back to Charlie, "Not that far. We're almost there."

All three boys had been good friends for years and were all about the same height and maturity. Jonathan Mitchell led the way. He was the heaviest, a little chubby with a round face, pale skin, and short blonde hair neatly combed. His father was the pastor of a small church, and Jonathan lived up to expectations by always behaving well.

In the middle of the line was a quieter and meeker boy with a small frame and freckled nose, Scott Taverns. Jonathan led the boys, flamboyantly projecting his knowledge, while Scott remained reserved, having a reputation for sensitivity and courtesy.

At the end of the line, Charlie Wolf, the most fit and athletic of the three, walked sluggishly with his arms folded and his eyes looking upward indicating that Jonathan's blabbering annoyed him.

Suddenly Jonathan stopped while Charlie and Scott slowly walked to his side to look where he directed his eyes. Jonathan stared at a thick tree that had stood in the same place for hundreds of years. Moss hung off the branches, giving it a haunted appearance.

Jonathan proudly smiled, "There it is."

Charlie, his arms still folded, pointed a finger upward to give himself permission to speak, "So there are Indians buried in there?"

"Yep. Their ghosts haunt this tree."

"Let's try to open the trunk," said Charlie as he quickly grabbed a heavy thick branch off the ground. Moving to the tree, he started striking it hard, as hard as he could. The bark would not budge as the tree refused to respond.

Charlie kept swinging at the tree whining, "Why won't it do anything?"

Scott walked up and spoke above the sound of the heavy branch hitting the trunk, "You can't use a branch to open the tree."

Charlie stopped swinging and wiped the sweat from his eyes, looking embarrassed.

The boys were all startled as a man appeared in the woods hollering, "Boys! What are you doing to my favorite tree?"

All three boys froze, hearts thumping in their ears. Not realizing they were on the man's property and that the man was actually speaking in a friendly tone, Jonathan shouted, "Run!"

The order sent them all dashing through the woods as fast as their legs could carry them. A few minutes later, they arrived in an open grassy area where they collapsed, gasping for air. A soft breeze blew over them, as they sprawled on their backs on the grass. When their hearts had stopped racing and as they all gazed upward at the sky, Scott spoke, "I'm glad we're all friends."

Jonathan replied, "We'll be friends forever. I can just feel it."

# CHAPTER 2

On a November day thirty-two years later, a cool, dry breeze brushed the trees on the edge of a Florida golf course. Florida had mostly evergreens, so the trees never changed with the seasons, and the weather didn't change much either.

*Whack!* A golf ball soared down the fairway as a man held his club over his shoulder with one hand while sheltering his eyes from the sun with the other. The ball arched high and landed with a soft thump in a sand trap near the green. The golfer dropped his club and shook his head.

"Let's see if Charlie can do better," a voice spoke as the embarrassed golfer turned around. Everyone watched as Charlie Wolf confidently approached the tee. He was in his mid-forties with dark brown hair cut short and styled with a small cowlick in the front. Anyone could tell by looking at his haircut that he went to an expensive hair salon. His face was slightly aged, but he still retained his good looks. He was tall with a fine build. Lifting weights every day of the week had paid off.

Charlie placed the golf ball on the grass and positioned himself to the side of it adjusting his fingers on the club. He looked down, then at his target, then down again, swung the club back, and propelled the ball smoothly. The ball went soaring as Charlie and the others looked on in silence. The ball landed right on the green.

The three men started cheering, "Nice job, Wolfie."

Charlie smiled awkwardly as he walked towards them speaking, "That's what happens when you get a promotion."

The three men joined in a masculine, mechanical laugh. Charlie continued, "Hey, what do you say we all have a drink after this?"

Charlie and his golf buddies walked inside their favorite bar in the city, *The Verona*. It was a place for nightlife, for friends and singles to mingle. The atmosphere was dark with flashing colored lights whirling around the stage where a DJ sat with huge speakers and countless CDs, mostly techno music. *The Verona* was a popular place not only because it had music, dancing, and lounging, but there was no membership and no cover charge.

Cigarette smoke clouded the place and tall mugs of cold, golden beer were on tables all around the room. The stuffy room was packed with people, mostly young and single. It was loud and the techno beat vibrated through everything, making it hard to socialize in this social club.

When Charlie walked in, a few heads turned and several people stood to shake his hand. Charlie had a contagious, friendly countenance, a remarkable memory for people's names making it clear that he even remembered something personal about each one.

Every few steps, someone would approach Charlie, and he took the time to speak to each person who spoke to him, "…Hey, I watched the Gators play last night…I'm sorry about what happened…Hey Stan, I still remember…Pete buddy, still have your DVD. I'll return it tomorrow…"

Finally, after shaking numerous cold, wet hands, Charlie made his way to the bar for a drink. He leaned on his elbows, greeted the two men next to him, and the bartender turned around, "Wolfie my man! What can I get you?"

Charlie smiled, teeth flashing, "Surprise me today."

"Sure thing," the bartender was eager to please.

Charlie continued leaning on his elbows, waiting patiently, while bobbing his head to the music. He turned his head to see who he might have missed as he entered.

Behind him, he spotted two very attractive women, apparently part of a group of singles. He looked at one of them long enough for her to notice and make eye contact.

Charlie could not take his eyes off of her. Though not old looking, Charlie was still classified as an "older man" in *The Verona*, but with his good looks and gregarious personality, he earned admiration quickly.

The woman could tell Charlie was one of those older men, perhaps one of those wealthy older men, the kind of man who could offer some security. She walked up to the bar gracefully and squeezed in between Charlie and the man next to him. Though she pretended she had not noticed Charlie, it was obvious to Charlie that she had noticed him.

Charlie immediately commented, "I like your necklace."

The woman looked at him and smiled, "Thanks."

They talked for twenty minutes about nothing important. Finally, she said she better get going, and Charlie asked for and got her phone number.

Charlie liked to have a bunch of phone numbers. He wanted to be prepared in case he ever got lonely and needed a date.

❦          ❦          ❦

A rather large traditional church stood in a small town on the flat Florida terrain. It was a simple church design with a steeple, front doors, and a plain rectangular sanctuary behind large front doors. It was not a dead church, a struggling church, or a fancy church. It was just a simple church with the same people sitting in the pews every Sunday singing from the sun-damaged hymnals that had a copyright of 1963. Going to church was routine and expected. Gossip among church members was contagious, as was true with so many other churches as well.

This Sunday was different. Everyone watched intently as a new man walked up to the pulpit. The man wore a nice new suit with an expensive red tie. He had fair skin that looked like it could burn easily in the sun and a round chubby face. He was tall, heavy, and had thin blonde hair tightly combed across his head.

He eyed the congregation, then spoke with a deep, booming, professional voice, as if he was on the campaign trail, "Praise the Lord for this church."

His voice was low and raspy when he said it. He lifted his shoulders and straightened his back, speaking even louder but more cheerfully, "Can I hear an amen?"

The congregation responded pleasantly, "Amen."

The man smiled and continued, "My name is Dr. Jonathan Mitchell and I am thrilled and honored to follow in the footsteps of Reverend Theodore. I grew up in a small town in Florida with two younger brothers. Our father pastored a small church. At the age of eighteen God called me to into the ministry. After eight years of studying biblical theology, I received my doctorate. I've worked under the ministry of the People of God for fifteen years helping churches grow under the leadership of our Father. And now I'm here with you at the First Baptist Church to help all of us to grow not just in numbers, but especially as individuals for the glory of God.

"When I walked in this church for the first time to meet your pastor, I was immediately overwhelmed by the spiritual strength of the people and the blessing that God has poured out on all of you. I would like to thank Reverend Theodore for honoring me by recommending me as your new pastor. But more importantly, I thank God for choosing me to fill this important position, as evidenced by your enthusiastic call. I would also like to thank God for leading Reverend Theodore in a new direction to do extraordinary things for His Kingdom. Thank you and God bless you."

With an assuring nod and a tight-lipped smile, Jonathan shook hands with Reverend Theodore as the whole congregation stood in applause.

*Ring!* The bell finally rung, as the anxious high school students shuffled their trumpets, flutes, clarinets, and other wind instruments. There were no school uniforms, as this was a public high school. The clothes were a mix, reflecting different preferences by race and socio-economic status; but all of the students shared a unity in their passion for music.

"Alright, nice work today. Tomorrow we're going to start off with *Carol of the Bells* so be ready, it's not easy," said the music teacher.

Scott Taverns was a man in his forties with healthy brown wavy hair that was parted on the side. He was medium in height and weight and was a classic looking man. Slacks and a tie were his dress code every day. He did not get paid much as a teacher, but he had a devotion to music and a quiet personality, making it easy to endure the life of a music teacher.

Band was not a highly respected class in a high school of this size, so Mr. Taverns did not get the nicest classroom. It was somewhat small, cramped and old. The air conditioner unit often malfunctioned. The room had the mildew stench of an old used classroom that had not been maintained. While Mr. Taverns was not the most organized man, he was neat, so everything in his room was arranged perfectly, and his desk was organized and clean.

Scott Taverns walked slowly towards his swivel desk chair, turned around, put his hands on his knees, and sat down heavily, exhausted from the day. It was 3:00 and it was Friday. It was now November right before Thanksgiving, and Scott was busy working on the Christmas school production, filled with Christmas songs, poems, and a word from the principal. Scott's musical talents were only needed on special occasions: the fall play, the Christmas production, and the spring play.

The telephone rang.

Scott picked up, "This is Scott Taverns."

A deep enthusiastic voice he did not recognize replied, "Hey Scott, this is Jonathan Mitchell."

The name immediately rang a bell in Scott's mind. Jonathan Mitchell. He narrowed his eyes searching his memory. Oh, one of his good friends as a kid! He gasped in surprise, "Oh, Jonathan. Yes, of course I remember you. Gosh, it's been a long time. How have you been?"

Jonathan laughed with delight, "Oh I've been doing great, Scott. How have you been?"

"I'm a music teacher now."

"Oh really?"

"Yeah. What are you doing now? Still church stuff?"

Jonathan's voice slowed to his theological tone, "Well I wouldn't call it church stuff. It's ministry. I actually became pastor of the First Baptist Church last summer."

"Oh really? Wow, that's great." Scott wasn't surprised. There was an awkward pause. Why would this guy I haven't seen in ten years be calling me? "Is there something I need to know about?"

Scott heard lips smack as Jonathan replied, "Well I'm glad you asked that, Scott. I would like to discuss a position at my church with you. I've prayed that God would send us the right person, and as I prayed the Lord just kept on saying to me, '*Scott Taverns, Scott Taverns.*'"

Scott lowered his eyebrows in a confused and disbelieving way, as he thought to himself: "Is this what happens to a guy who grows up in the church with a pastor dad? What could Jonathan Mitchell possibly want from me after all these years? How can someone like me work for a church?" Scott was speechless.

Jonathan noticed the prolonged silence and said, "I would really like to talk with you, Scott. Can you meet me at Starbucks tomorrow at ten o' clock?"

"Um, let's see, ten o' clock, ten o' clock," he mumbled to himself as he shuffled through his calendar to see if he was busy. He had nothing planned. He reluctantly replied, "I'm free tomorrow. I have nothing scheduled tomorrow morning."

"Good," Jonathan sounded pleased, "ten o'clock tomorrow then."

Scott pressed his lips together and nodded, "Ten o'clock, I'll be there."

"Okay, good."

"Well I'll see you tomorrow. Have a nice rest of the day."

Jonathan's voice softened as he spoke in a fatherly voice, "You too, Scott. God bless."

As he hung up, Scott leaned back in his chair. He was a little anxious about what Jonathan was going to say to him, but whatever it was, he was open and he was looking forward to seeing his old friend again.

# CHAPTER 3

The apartment door opened. Charlie Wolf sighed comfortably. Home sweet home. It was a roomy expensive apartment with contemporary furniture and lots of high tech features. The first sight from the door was the clean, spacious, white kitchen. The silver Sub-Zero refrigerator, the silver dishwasher, the glass blender, the sharp imported knives, and the state-of-the-art silver espresso machine were all there, perfectly placed. It was about 6:30, as the sun was setting and beaming in through the windows illuminating the tiny dust particles.

The floor was a light hardwood. An opening in the kitchen wall allowed a view of the modern comfortable living room with leather sofas and modern art on the walls. White and blue were the primary colors in Charlie's home. There were some cubism art pieces on the walls and a few funky objects scattered about, but the style was mainly simple, modern and expensive.

Charlie walked slowly towards the white leather sofa in front of the wide screen TV, picked up the remote control from the end table and stretched out. The room was silent as he turned on an easy listening CD in his stereo system bought on a European vacation. For a moment he stared at the wall, but then a smile formed on his face and he quietly snickered for no reason. He was single, he was wealthy, he had everything he wanted, he had influential friends, he had respect, he had people, he had fun, and he had the best home. What more could he ask for? Life was perfect for him and he felt sorry for everyone else in the world. He had gone on a date with a woman he met at *The Verona* a few weeks earlier, but that had not worked out; she was long forgotten.

*Ring!* Charlie shifted himself on the sofa and reached for the telephone on the table.

"Hello?"

"Charlie, where are you?" asked a woman.

Charlie rolled his eyes and sunk back in the sofa with the telephone against his ear. He despised hearing the voice of his ex-wife, Diane. He moaned as if this day was the most stressful day of his life, "Oh gosh, I totally forgot. It totally slipped my mind." He really had forgotten.

Diane let out a frustrated sigh and spoke firmly, "Franklin has been waiting here for an hour and a half. And where have you been?"

Charlie opened his mouth trying to search for a better answer but simply repeated himself, "I already told you. I just forgot. It's been a long hard day at work, and I totally forgot."

It was Friday. Every Friday at 5:00, Charlie picked up his twelve-year-old son, Franklin for some father/son time. It was part of the divorce arrangement and he was fully aware of this. Diane wanted to blow up on the phone, but she could not with Franklin in the house. Instead, she inhaled and exhaled a few times until Charlie finally said, "What are you doing? Are you working out?"

The breathing stopped as she fired back, "No, Charlie, I'm just trying to keep from losing my temper."

He said sarcastically, "Well I have no idea what you've been up to lately."

She snapped back in a loud whisper, "Charlie, this is a brainless conversation. Just come over here, pick up your son, and be happy for his sake. Okay?"

Charlie answered nodding his head, "Okay I will."

"Okay, good. Bye." She hung up abruptly.

Charlie hung up and slowly lifted himself from the sofa and stretched his arms. See, this is why you don't get married. If you ever want to leave your wife, you have to carry a bunch of baggage and your whole past with you. The hard earned alimony payments go to a lady you can't stand. Serious relationships are not worth it. He repeated these thoughts every time he talked to Diane. Charlie grabbed his Mercedes keys and locked the door behind him.

❦          ❦          ❦

Scott was in his car behind a red light on a Saturday morning. He checked his watch. 10:10. He was running ten minutes late in meeting one of his best childhood buddies. He made a right turn into the parking lot where he saw the green sign with the round logo with some kind of mermaid in the middle he had never understood, *"STARBUCKS COFFEE."* He took a quick look in the tall windows and saw the usual middle-aged men drinking hot beverages while reading the newspaper or discussing business.

His heart started thumping a little faster as he turned off his motor and got out. "I haven't seen Jonathan in years. What could he want from me?"

Scott wore khaki pants and a blue sweater since the temperature outside was getting colder at this time of year. He opened the door, smiled as he held it open for a woman behind him, and walked in. The Starbucks workers were busy in their green aprons running the squeaky espresso machines and hollering out drink orders.

After taking a music course in France over the summer, Scott had a whole new perspective on the efficiency of American culture. The French, he observed, spent hours eating food every day. Time did not matter to them. When he came back home at the end of July, the frenetic pace of every day life in America was overwhelming to him. He was distressed by the spectacle of American restaurants packing as many people in as possible, then giving the remaining customers vibrating, flashy devices to hold until a new table became available. When you finally do get a table, the servers rush in your order and rush you out as fast as they can.

Productivity and efficiency are the two principles by which American culture lives. If Scott wanted a cup of coffee in France, that meant sitting down, sipping it, and eventually asking for the check. In his own America, however, the cashier rings quickly as a constant flow of people are herded through with coffee in cardboard to-go cups.

Scott stood and looked around the room trying to spot a familiar face. One face was obviously looking right back at him. Sure enough, it was Jonathan. Scott smiled, pointed at him, and laughed in a friendly way, "Ha, it's you!"

Jonathan smiled and laughed in reply as he stood and walked towards him. They shook hands, "It's good to see you, brother."

Scott smiled back, "Good to see you too."

"Do you want a drink or anything?"

"Well I was just planning to have a cappuccino," he replied as he moved towards the counter.

"No, no, let me pay for it," Jonathan insisted.

"No, it's fine, I'll pay for it."

"I brought you here, I'll get you a cappuccino."

There was no point in arguing, so Scott gave in, "Okay fine, you can pay for it."

Jonathan ordered cappuccinos for both, paid, and they sat at a table to talk.

Scott began by answering questions about his life since he had last seen Jonathan. He talked about where his major in music had taken him, his studying in France last summer, his teaching and the Christmas production he was currently working on at the public high school.

Then it was Jonathan's turn to share his story about his ministry and successful churches he had planted and how God had blessed him, finishing with the local church he was now pastoring. Scott found Jonathan's story surprisingly interesting.

They talked about shared past experiences and memories. They laughed as they recalled stories of their childhood and the people they knew and the neighbors they had spied on and found other ways to irritate, including the old man and the tree with Indians buried in it.

"Have you talked to Charlie too?" asked Scott.

Jonathan immediately shook his head, "No, no," he paused, "but I've heard about him. He has a young son, and he's divorced."

Scott was a little shocked, "Oh really? How come no one tells me this stuff?"

Jonathan shrugged, "I don't know. I didn't know about it until recently. It happened about two years ago."

"Well what caused the divorce?"

Jonathan lowered his head so that he looked up into Scott's eyes and said the word like it was a classified document, "Adultery." He paused, "He had an affair with a co-worker."

"Gosh, that's terrible."

Jonathan nodded in agreement, "Yes, it's very sad, and he has a young son too. I don't know what he's doing right now, but I know that he is straying from God. We really need to pray for him."

Scott nodded, "Okay."

Jonathan switched to a more cheerful tone as he changed the subject, "Well I still need to tell you why I wanted to meet with you."

Scott leaned in.

"The First Baptist Church lacks strong worship on Sundays. Currently, we sing traditional hymns. I want to make worship more exciting and attractive to younger people. I've heard all about you, Scott, and you are young, energetic, and talented. I would like to recommend you to the church as Minister of Worship at First Baptist."

Scott's eyes widened in surprise, "So you want me to lead the music every Sunday?"

Jonathan nodded, "Yes and it would be great to expand our worship through drama, concerts, ways that are more creative. I know you have the potential and a musical talent from God."

"So I would have to leave my current job at the school?"

"Well yes, but you can finish up the school year and we can start next summer. I'm not pressuring you. You don't have to take this job if you don't want to, but you do have a gift, Scott, and we need to use our gifts to glorify God. You don't have to decide right now. This is just something to pray about."

Scott was flattered, excited, anxious, but unconvinced at the moment, "Okay, I'll think about it."

The kitchen of the Mitchell's charming house was alive with conversation, laughter, and happiness. Jonathan carried on a conversation with his brother-in-law while his mother, his mother-in-law, and all the women in the house worked to prepare the meal and manned the ovens.

They chatted, shared stories, laughed, and smiled. There were young children and Jonathan's two daughters who were in their early twenties. Grandpa sat in a chair on the living room sofa watching and smiling over his grandchildren playing on the floor. A worship CD played in the stereo system. The small two-story house was brand new and mostly empty so far. The living room by the kitchen had some furniture and lamps in place, but the other rooms were empty with items still in boxes that were against the walls. The kitchen was completely done and the dining table was big and had been set up. The Mitchells purposely did not have a TV because they considered most programs to be "trash."

Jonathan's wife, Sara, pulled the full-sized turkey out of the oven exclaiming excitedly, "Who's ready for the turkey?"

Sara was a pleasant woman in her mid-thirties with an outgoing personality and positive attitude. Her blonde hair was short and styled.

The kitchen conversation was so loud that only the people close by could hear her. They replied in "oohs" and "ahhs," "That looks delicious!"

The women placed the turkey, sweet potatoes, corn casserole, squash, chicken stuffing, gravy, and rolls on the table. The children started gathering around the food as the adults gradually made their way towards the table complementing the cooks.

When the talking died down, Jonathan spoke, "Let's go to our Father in thanksgiving."

Everyone bowed their heads, closed their eyes, and held hands in a circle.

Jonathan continued, "Our Heavenly Father, we give you so much thanks for our family and for this time for us to come together for fellowship. While we do enjoy and cherish each other, more importantly, we thank you for everything you have blessed us with and for each member of this family."

There were quiet sounds of agreement from several people at the table in reply to the last phrase.

"And we thank you for our country, for our freedom, and for our ability to worship you. Bless everyone here in every step in life they go through. I pray for the First Baptist Church and I pray that you will use me as a tool to help the church grow. Thank You, thank You, thank You, Lord. In Your Son Jesus' name we pray. Amen."

Everyone repeated the "amen" while some of the women wiped tears from their eyes moved by the prayer and the feeling of a big family spending time together. Sara turned her head towards him, "Thank you Jonathan. That was beautiful."

They all started eating, as Jonathan's brother turned to him with food in his mouth, "So how's the church going?"

Jonathan finished chewing and then replied, "It's going very well so far. It has already grown in size. Lately I've been on a search trying to find a new Music Director, and I felt the Lord placing Scott Taverns on my heart. I met with him last weekend."

Sara already knew about the meeting, but Jonathan's parents and his two siblings were bug-eyed with surprise at hearing a familiar name, "Scott Taverns?"

"Yep."

"How did you get in touch with him?" asked his mother.

"Well I knew he lived down here so I just looked in the phone book."

His brother spoke, "I would like to see old Scott again. It's been so long."

"Yeah, I think he has a lot of talent and potential for this church," said Jonathan.

There was an awkward pause. Finally, Jonathan's sister's eleven-year-old son abruptly changed the subject, "Hey I have a girlfriend now."

His mother, who was sitting next to him, looked down and squeezed his arm embarrassed. She looked up and laughed clarifying for him, "She's not your girlfriend."

He objected, "Mom, yes she is."

Jonathan spoke, "Well I told my two daughters when they were younger that I'm the only man in their life right now until they're in college."

There were a few laughs in reply. After eating and talking, the Mitchell family sat down in the living room where they played a game of Bible trivia and then afterwards they each went around in a circle saying what they were particularly thankful for.

The Taverns family was also very cheerful and family-oriented on Thanksgiving. They were traditional like the Mitchells, had the turkey and all the other Thanksgiving food, and had all the parents, siblings, nieces, and nephews over. They went around telling what they were thankful for, but they never said a blessing or did anything spiritual like the Mitchell family.

The doorbell rang in the nice, pretty, well-kept house. It was rather big with a classic, symmetrical, colonial design and a beautiful landscape. It was evening and the walkway lamps lighted the brick path to the front door. Diane Wolf opened the door to find Charlie, hands in pockets, looking the same as always, including the closed lips and fake smile on his face. Next to Charlie stood their son, Franklin, with his dark hair and child-like features.

Diane was an attractive woman in her thirties wearing very stylish clothing and medium length blonde hair in a professional businesswoman fashion. She ran her fingers through her hair, pressed her lips together, and said simply, "Hey."

Charlie responded with an equal amount of enthusiasm, "Hey. Just returning Frankie to you."

She nodded, "How was lunch?"

He tried to be bright, "It was really good. We had turkey, cranberry sauce, stuffing." He turned to Franklin and smiled, "Well how did you like it?"

Franklin nodded, "It was really good."

"Tonight we're going to visit my parents," Diane said.

Charlie replied, "Oh."

Diane pulled Franklin by the arm inside and spoke to him with a lighter tone in her voice, "Well are you ready to go?" Once Franklin was inside, Diane turned back to Charlie as she was closing the door, "Well goodbye Charlie."

Charlie put on his fake smile again and waved sheepishly, "Good—"

But before he could finish his goodbye, Diane apparently did not like his expression, so she closed the door in his face. Charlie stood in front of the door with his hand still up waving. He finally put it down and started walking back to his car muttering to himself.

# CHAPTER 4

Hot humidity swept through the Florida summer air. Gnats and mosquitoes buzzed around and preyed on any creature that was outside. It was early Monday afternoon at the First Baptist Church as the church workers were busy in their small offices. The temperature was in the upper eighties and the air-conditioning system was not working, so portable fans were buzzing in every office.

The double doors at the other end of the sanctuary across from the platform opened as Scott and Jonathan walked in. Jonathan led as Scott followed him down the center aisle with wooden pews on either side. Jonathan raised his hands up as if he was advertising a brand new hotel lobby, "This is our beautiful sanctuary."

Scott followed while looking around curiously, "Wow, it's beautiful."

It was not a huge spectacular site, but it was a nice church sanctuary and several hundred people could sit comfortably in the pews. The lights were off and it was hot. Scott visualized the sanctuary with the lights turned on, the congregation, the pastor, and the music. He was suddenly excited about his new position. A chandelier hung from a high arched ceiling, the side windows were tall, the stage was roomy, but Scott paid particular attention to the technology necessary for producing a decent musical production. The lighting was professional, there was a nice sound box in the back corner, and the sound acoustics were good quality.

Jonathan was rambling about the church. He stopped midway down the aisle, put his hand on one of the pews to rest and faced Scott, "This sanctuary was built nineteen years ago, but it's been remodeled a few times. This carpet is brand new and all the technical mechanics are updated. We have a full choir, an organist, pianist, keyboard player, bass player, everything you would need."

Satisfaction filled Scott as he smiled, "Actually I've been thinking about this lately and I have a vision to do a huge Christmas production with drama and music. It'd be wonderful; I have it all set up in my mind."

A smile of pleasure appeared on Jonathan's face, "Well good, we would support you in every way. We will do anything to reach people with the Gospel." He paused and then changed the subject, "I want you to meet some of the people who work in the music department here."

"Okay." With that, they walked on and continued talking.

❧          ❧          ❧

The church offered Scott the position as Music Director. After pondering this new job opportunity for some time, Scott had decided to take it. His first Sunday morning approached.

An organ played as the regular churchgoers were moving to their seats socializing before the service started. Scott sat in a chair up on the platform dressed casually with his heart beating fast in his chest. *Just calm down. You've lead music many times before.* Reverend Mitchell sat in a chair to the left of him on the other side of the pulpit with the assistant pastor. His wife, Sara, was sitting in the front row looking at him admiringly.

Finally, the organist ended on a loud long note with all of her ten fingers on the keys. As the organ fell silent, everyone sat down quietly while Jonathan walked up to the pulpit, smiled, and spoke in a booming voice, "Good morning."

The congregation replied at once, "Good morning."

Jonathan put his hands on his hips playfully, "Oh, come on, you can do better than that!" There was a low chuckle in the pews. "Let me try again. Good morning!"

"Good morning!" the congregation said louder.

"That's better. If you read the announcements in your bulletin this morning, you read about our new Music Director at First Baptist. I have known Scott Taverns since we were little kids. We used to play together all the time, and I remember one time as a child, Scott told me that church reminded him of a haunted house when the organ played." Jonathan turned to the organist who was sitting on the organ bench smiling, "No offense Morgan."

People laughed, including Morgan, the organist.

Jonathan continued with a jolly attitude, "And Scott still thinks that."

Scott's face turned red as he joined the laughter of the congregation all looking his way.

"Scott is here to take the music ministry to a new level in this church. He wants to satisfy those who are thirsty for Jesus Christ and who want to worship Him in Spirit and in truth."

A few serious sounds emanated from the pews.

Jonathan continued, "After earning his doctorate in music, Scott has had many experiences in his chosen profession, including being part of a technical crew for musical productions, performing and singing with his guitar, and most recently, Scott has been the music teacher at our local high school. With utmost confidence, I know that God will use you, Scott, to fulfill His calling on your life.

And without further adieu, I would like to take this opportunity to introduce you all to our Music Director, Scott Taverns."

The congregation applauded with Jonathan as he turned towards Scott who stood and walked to him and shook his hand. As he took a seat in a front row pew, Jonathan mouthed an encouraging, "God bless you."

Scott picked up his guitar and put the strap around his shoulder, as the rest of the band positioned themselves to play. Scott made eye contact with each band member before he strummed his guitar. The keyboardist immediately joined him on a low chord. As the tone resounded through the sanctuary, Scott spoke, "Let's lift up our voices."

As Scott strummed his guitar rhythmically, the drummer set a beat, and a few members of the congregation could be heard joining in as they clapped to the beat. Scott, two other male singers, and two female singers led from the platform in a familiar, contemporary worship song. Scott managed to eye the worshippers in the pews, attempting to get a sense of the influence his musical leadership was having. Most of the elderly people stood, but kept their lips tight trying to fathom this new music. The younger people recognized the song and sang along. Scott led a few more worship songs and then he and the band sat down while the congregation applauded.

The two plates full of food, the glasses, and the silverware were already set in place as Jonathan and Sara sat down at their wooden dining table. Jonathan sat at the head where he had always sat in all the years of his marriage and parenting. This was a reflection of his and Sara's view of his position as head of the home. In the chair next to him, Sara sat in front of a big square window that reflected their images and the lighted kitchen behind them because of the darkness outside.

By habit, Sara joined her husband when he bowed his head. He prayed, "Our Heavenly Father, we thank you for this blessed Sunday and for the new position you have put Scott in. I ask that you be with Scott not only as he leads the church in music, but also in everyday life in his walk with you. I pray for our two daughters as they study Your Word and bless them, Lord, as they enter in ministry to spread your gospel to the world. Thank you for everything you have blessed us with. Bless the food to make us better prepared for your service. In Jesus' name I pray. Amen."

With that, they picked up their forks and started eating. Jonathan spoke, "It's kind of lonely without the girls here eating with us."

Sara finished chewing her bite adding, "And quiet."

"Yep."

Sara took another bite and chewed it, "I talked to Michelle at church this morning. And do you know what she told me? Denise's oldest son was expelled for doing drugs."

Jonathan looked at her and shook his head, "Oh my goodness. Where was he when he did it?"

"Well he was at a party. And you know how those go now?"

He admitted, "I cannot believe how corrupt this world is now. I hope and pray that Kristi and Lauren are not around those kinds of people right now."

"Well, this is why we put them into Christian colleges."

"True, but it's still around. It's just not as much at Christian College."

"I'm going to call Lauren tonight and see what she's doing. I think we need to talk about the peer pressure and temptations that everyone faces in college."

Sara nodded and agreed, "Okay."

"I want you to call Kristi up in Virginia and have the same kind of talk with her."

"That's a good idea."

She changed the subject, "We need to pray for Nathan and Ann."

"Why?"

"They're having some marriage problems, and it's really sad."

Jonathan's eyes dropped sorrowfully, "Hmm, that's terrible." He paused and then stated, "God has really worked in the hearts of the women in your Bible study today. A lot of prayer power is going on right now."

Sara lowered her chin and raised her eyebrows, "And that's not all. Louis' son is in alcohol rehab. Tom's middle daughter totaled her car and then blamed her parents for giving her the car in the first place. Samantha is quitting her job as head of administration at her Christian school because she doesn't agree with some of the new rules in the dress code. So now, she's trying to find a new job, so we need to really keep her in our prayers. Rachel and Rick recently got a divorce, and because of a little quarrel they had, the selfish man didn't pay the electricity bill. So Rachel and her three small children had no electricity for days!"

Jonathan pursed his lips and shook his head, "It breaks my heart to hear about all this happening in our church. We really need to pray for these people."

🍁          🍁          🍁

Charlie spent some time on the Internet searching for the best seafood restaurant in town. Jean's Fish Market had the highest ratings and was featured in a monthly magazine. So now here he was sitting in an elegant restaurant in a small booth designed for two people with a pretty single woman across from him. He took the wineglass by the stem and sipped the little bit of wine remaining, tossing it in his mouth trying to absorb the full flavor. He swallowed, eyed the waiter, and nodded.

After the waiter refilled the two wineglasses with red wine and left, Charlie looked at the attractive woman across from him. Her blue eye shadow brought out her blue eyes and her red lipstick made her lips look soft and delicate. Charlie gave her a flirtatious smile, "Red wine helps the food digest."

She acted interested, "Oh, I didn't know that." For a few seconds, they darted their eyes around the restaurant awkwardly until Charlie broke the silence, "So are you the only child in your family?"

"Yeah," she replied, "I was a spoiled child. I—"

As she was speaking, an electronic tune rang obnoxiously in Charlie's pocket. He rolled his eyes reaching for his pocket to see who was calling. The caller ID identified *"Diane."* He quickly turned off his cell phone. He apologized, "Sorry for that."

"Who was that?" she asked.

He hesitated, waving his hand and then replied off-handedly, "Oh it's just someone at work. Go ahead with what you were saying."

"Oh it was nothing important."

He lowered his eyebrows and reached across the table to rub her arm playfully, "Oh come on, you were going to say something."

She laughed sweetly, "I was just going to say that I was spoiled."

Resting his hand on her arm, Charlie moved in closer to her as their eyes connected. The reflection of the candle flame danced in her eyes.

As they spoke quietly, something suddenly caught Charlie's eye right over his date's head. He glanced up to see his ex-wife who had just walked in.

Charlie did his best to hide the fact he had seen Diane, taking his hand off his date's arm, and brushing his eyebrow with his fingers hoping to cover his face with his hand.

His date continued the conversation, apparently oblivious to the situation, "How long have you been working in the business? You seem like you know exactly what you're doing all the time."

Charlie tried to maintain his composure as he kept his fingers on his eyebrow, "Um, I've been working there for ten years now." He moved his eyes to Diane who stood there looking straight at him, signaling him with her finger to come to her. He did not budge, hoping she would soon give up.

"Wow, that's a long time," she replied.

He glanced again, and this time Diane started making her way towards him. He stood up hastily and said, "Would you excuse me for a second? I need to go to the restroom."

He left the table and walked up to Diane. He stood in front of her with his hands on his hips and said, "What?"

She stood there sternly and spoke as though her being there was completely by obligation, "You still haven't given me money to pay for Franklin's horse lessons."

Charlie let out a heavy frustrating sigh and rolled his eyes, "Is this why you came all the way over here? Did you follow me?"

"Well I need to pay and it's not my problem that I haven't had the money."

"Couldn't you just wait and call me?"

"I tried calling your cell phone and you didn't pick it up."

"That's because I was having dinner." Charlie turned his head around and saw the back of his date's head as she sat calmly putting on another coat of lipstick.

Diane tilted her head in the direction on his booth and folded her arms, "And who's that?"

"That's just a business acquaintance. And that is not your business, Diane, and I don't have time for this." He spoke more forcefully but quietly, "You need to find something better to do with your time and do things that are more productive than chasing me around the city reminding me of pointless nonsense."

She spoke back with the same intensity stabbing her finger in her chest, "I have a child to support!"

"Okay Ms. Women's-Rights-Movement, and I have to make money to support your child. I really don't have time for this, I'm leaving now." As he turned around to go back to his seat, he saw his date standing up and walking towards him with her purse over her shoulder.

Her lips were pressed together as she stomped quickly towards him. She boldly asked, "Who is this?"

Charlie was just about to sprint out of the restaurant as these two devils stared at him causing a scene. He held out his hand like he was presenting something, "This is Ms. Wolf."

His date gasped, "You're married?"

"No, I used to be married," he corrected.

"Well you never told me that."

His face was baffled as he raised his voice, "Well I was going to tell you that. And did you really expect a gray-haired guy like me to have never been married?"

Tears welled in her eyes as she spoke trembling, "I thought you were someone different."

Charlie still appeared baffled, "Well that shouldn't change anything. It doesn't matter if I've been married or—"

She snapped back responding, "Yes, Charlie. As a matter of fact, it does. You were hiding that for three months now and you did a pretty good job. You're great at deceiving."

"Deceiving? Look, I—"

She put her hand up signaling an end to the conversation as she managed to get the last word, "I don't want to talk to you right now." With that, she left Jean's Fish Market.

Charlie and Diane both stared at the door in silence and then he turned around to look at all the faces looking right at him. He did not care about being noticed anymore; it was too late anyway. He looked at Diane who just shrugged. He was upset, so he was not ashamed to talk louder.

Curling his fingers like claws, he yelled, "What is your goal? To ruin my life? Can you find something else better to do?"

She shrugged again leaning into his face fearlessly, "If you wouldn't play around with so many women, all your problems would be fixed. You brought it upon yourself."

"You just need to grow up and stop acting like some teenager."

Diane started walking toward the door while speaking over her shoulder, "Oh, and who's the adolescent?"

Charlie snarled back loudly, "Yeah, get a life!"

She closed the door and Charlie found himself standing in a public place with every eye upon him. Some people tried to be polite and resume eating, some kept staring, and some laughed mockingly as if to say, "He deserved that." Charlie looked down at the floor, as he was flooded with an overwhelming sense of insecurity.

*       *       *

It was Sunday; Pastor Mitchell stood behind his pulpit preaching. The congregation listened intently with their Bibles open.

Jonathan preached, "In 1 Corinthians, Paul is criticizing the church for their corruption. Idolatry was becoming rampant."

Suddenly, right in the middle of Jonathan's sermon, the double doors opened directly at the back of the sanctuary. There stood a man dressed in dirty worn blue jeans and a ripped T-shirt revealing scars and burns on his chest and body. He was a large white man with a gruff face, grubby beard, and long course hair that frizzed like a classic image of a caveman.

Some heads turned around to look at him and when they did, they continued staring. Jonathan was fully aware of the man in the sanctuary, but he decided to ignore the situation for now. Without taking his eyes off of the man, Jonathan stammered, "So when Paul writes this letter to the church of Corinth—"

The man started walking down the aisle with the palm of his hand facing upward, stopping at each pew as he made his way down. He was asking for money. Jonathan noticed that on his left arm was a huge gruesome gash in the skin going from his shoulder to his wrist. The black, crusty, burned skin made a crater in his arm like a dessert. There was a canyon made by some serious burn scars.

Blood started pumping faster through Jonathan's heart. The sight of the black burn on the man's arm made his stomach nauseous and the fact that he was begging his church members for money was a problem. He stopped preaching as mumbling filled the sanctuary.

Jonathan gave the ushers in the back a nod. Once they got the signal, they calmly walked down the aisle, gathered around the man, and escorted him to the door.

The man protested and from the pulpit, it sounded to Jonathan like he was saying, "My little daughter…she's starving…I need money."

The ushers responded to his protests by grasping both of his arms behind his back. Trying their best to be dignified, they had to get rid of the beggar. Finally, after a lot of commotion, the ushers managed to get the man out of the sanctuary. The turmoil in the foyer ended when the double doors closed with an echo. The uncomfortable congregation murmured to each other.

Wiping sweat off his forehead, Jonathan seemed to regain his composure and continued with his sermon. At the next deacon's meeting, a proposal for security measures during church service was proposed and adopted.

# CHAPTER 5

It was another Sunday morning at the First Baptist Church. The attentive congregation filled the pews. The sanctuary was quiet as Pastor Mitchell's voice resounded through the room amplified by the small unobtrusive microphone pinned onto his collar.

He concluded his sermon with an emotional appeal, "Give and you will receive. Give and you will receive. If we give ourselves for the Kingdom of God and give all we have to Him, then we will receive more than we gave, givers will be blessed and not the one who is greedy and selfish in the eyes of the Lord."

Scott sat in the front pew where he always sat and felt bothered by today's sermon on giving and receiving. He couldn't help the uneasy questions that entered his mind, "Is that the way it works? Give and you will receive more than you gave?"

Jonathan continued, "And so now as we close and as we start passing around the offering plate, let us remember the words of our Lord when He said, 'It is more blessed to give than to receive.' Shall we pray?"

That was the signal for Scott, so he and the rest of his worship team quietly stepped up onto the stage and carefully prepared for more music. *"Give and you will receive."* As Pastor Mitchell prayed, Scott strummed a few chords on the guitar quietly to add a dramatic but serene flare to the prayer. When he heard the word, 'amen,' that was the signal to start singing a song as the offering plates started traveling through the churchgoers in the pews. Thanks to the sermon, the people maybe, just maybe, felt a stronger urge to drop a little more money in this time.

After the benediction and all but a few people had left, Scott spotted Jonathan Mitchell shaking someone's hand and then walking up to the pulpit to get his Bible. Scott sat in one of the chairs on the platform and continued to observe as the ushers huddled in the back counting the money from the offering plates. Jonathan was grinning as he turned to walk toward Scott. Scott stood up and walked towards Jonathan calling out to him, "Jonathan."

Jonathan looked up at Scott and smiled as he walked over closer, "Oh hey Scott. How are you?"

"I'm doing fine."

"Yeah, great morning this morning."

Scott nodded and agreed, "Yeah, it was." He hesitated trying to think of what he was going to say to his lifelong friend, to the pastor of this church, to the man who hired him and gave him his job. He asked politely, "Did people give more this morning?"

Jonathan answered, "So far, it looks that way."

Scott nodded, "Do you think it was because of the sermon?"

Jonathan's countenance and manner changed as he spoke a little more softly, almost secretly, "Well I don't know, Scott. I was just speaking the Word of God. This is why I'm here. It wasn't because of me; it was because of the Holy Spirit. The Holy Spirit spoke through me and the Holy Spirit spoke to the hearts of the people."

Still a little disturbed, Scott said nothing to indicate his feelings.

Jonathan smiled and patted Scott's arm, "I'll talk to you later, Scott." With that, he walked away waving and greeting people as he made his way out of the sanctuary.

🍁          🍁          🍁

Charlie sat at his spacious cherry desk in his rolling leather office chair. A window across from his desk looked out over the city. Behind him was a bookshelf with beautifully bound books he had collected through the years. A doorway next to the window opened into the hallway. The walls were white and the atmosphere of Charlie's office was bright, cool, and relaxing. His computer blinked with a screen saver slide show of beautiful mountain scenes; papers were scattered on his desk.

With a cup of coffee always nearby, Charlie worked in his long sleeve oxford shirt with the sleeves rolled up wearing a silk tie. He was concentrating on the report he was writing when he heard a knock on the door. Without looking up from his work he called out, "Come in."

The door opened and Charlie glanced over to see a very familiar older man with a baldhead wearing glasses and dressed impeccably in coat and tie. Seeing it was his boss, Charlie quickly stopped what he was working on and gave him his complete undivided attention as he rose from his chair, "Hello, Mr. Safino."

Mr. Safino replied as he shut the door behind him, "Hi Charlie." Mr. Safino stood for a moment and then pulled a chair from a corner and sat down right in front of Charlie's desk.

Charlie sat back down in his chair trying to look as undisturbed as he could. He knew that when Mr. Safino came into your office, it was going to be either great or terrible news, there was no in between. Mr. Safino opened his mouth and started, "Charlie, I really hate saying this to you. But let me start by saying that you have been a great worker and a great asset to this company."

Charlie's heart started to race. His boss had never said that before so this could not have been a raise like he initially had expected.

Mr. Safino continued, "But as you already know, this country is going through a huge recession and if we don't watch out, we could easily enter into a depression. While that is the big picture for our nation, this company is also experiencing difficulties. Our stock has declined dramatically, we are hugely in debt, and we are losing money. Our sales are at a record low, and if we don't do something about it, we are going to go bankrupt."

Charlie's wheels started turning. *Is this a strange build up to another promotion?*

Mr. Safino's looked down as he sighed, dreading what he was about to say, "Charlie, I hate doing this, but we are forced to layoff some of our employees. The board and I decided that this was the best approach right now." His eyes looked deeply into Charlie's and his face grew sorrowful, "I'm sorry."

Charlie's eyes widened in shock as his heart sank. The room was completely silent except for the ticking clock on a shelf. His face froze in disbelief as the impact of Mr. Safino's news began to sink in. Charlie was dumbfounded as he nervously shuffled the papers he had been working on. He just stared for a moment at his boss looking at him disbelievingly. Mr. Safino wasn't just his boss; he had always been his *friend*. Charlie found himself struggling to find words, "Mr. Safino. I—"

Mr. Safino interrupted, "It's okay Charlie. I have recommendations for you for other positions in other companies."

Charlie tried to find reassurance in these words as a million thoughts swam through his mind, "Yeah, but this is the best job I could ever hope to have."

He was trying to be as nice as possible, but Charlie could not hold back his emotions. His voice rose to an unexpected crescendo, "But Mr. Safino, I've been working for you for ten years. This is my life. This is what I live for! You can't take this away from me!"

Mr. Safino sounded like he was talking to a little child when he responded gently, "Charlie, I'm sorry."

"How could you do this to me? I thought we were friends. I thought you liked my work; you have promoted me so many times. What have I done wrong?"

Mr. Safino remained calm, "You didn't do anything wrong, Charlie. We just found it in our best interest to—"

"Do you know how much I have to go through now? You know how I live, Mr. Safino. You know I'm a divorced man with a son. I don't have anyone else to turn to. You know how hard I have to work to support my ex-wife and son." He was now standing.

Mr. Safino now stood too, appearing a little irritated, "Well I'm afraid, Charlie, that we don't study the employee's personal issues before we decide to lay them off. Look, you will be fine. You already have enough money to support your family for a long time, and I've already made it clear that I'm looking for other opportunities for you. Just take it like a man."

That made Charlie mad. Take it like a man? What does that mean anyway? Live without emotion? With a mixture of anger, guilt and shame, Charlie marched over to retrieve his coat and made a quick exit as he spoke more to himself than to his boss, "I can't take this." He sharply closed the door behind him, leaving his boss standing in his office.

❦        ❦        ❦

The telephone rang in the kitchen. Diane walked over and picked it up, "Hello?"

"Diane, something terrible just happened." Charlie's voice sounded troubled.

"What happened?" she asked in a monotone voice not hiding her disinterest.

He said it bluntly, "I was fired from my job."

At this, Diane was jarred. This could affect her, "What did you do?"

"I didn't do anything. They are just having a huge layoff and I'm a part of it."

"What are you going to do now?"

"I don't know what I'm going to do. Rob Safino is recommending me for other positions, but they won't pay what I've been getting."

While she wasn't pleased with the prospect, Diane was shrewd enough to respond with encouragement, "Well Charlie, you're going to just have to bite the bullet and take on another job with a lower salary."

There was a pause and then Charlie groaned, "I don't know."

"Where are you right now?"

"In the car."

"This happens to people all the time. You might as well make the best of it."

Charlie did not respond.

"Hello?" Diane tried to bring Charlie back into the conversation. There was no answer, then a dial tone. Charlie had hung up on her.

Jonathan walked through the First Baptist Church parking lot to his white Ford Explorer, started the engine, and moved toward the exit. On his way out, he put one hand on the steering wheel and used the other hand to dial his cell phone. As he placed it on his ear, he heard Sara's voice, "Hello?"

Jonathan smiled at hearing his wife's precious voice, "Hey honey. How was your day?"

Sara answered, "Well I'm glad to be back at home. I just ran some errands today. How was your day at work?"

"It was great. I'm on my way home right now. I'll be home in about fifteen minutes. Okay?"

"Okay."

"I love you sweetheart."

She replied, "I love you too."

"Okay bye." He ended his call, put his cell phone in his glove compartment, and put on a worship CD.

🍁          🍁          🍁

Charlie drove his Mercedes way over the speed limit and recklessly. He was gritting his teeth as emotions and thoughts went through his head. Why couldn't he just grow up and take bad things like a man? Everyone else had to go through the same sort of things. He felt ashamed at his behavior and realizing his own shame made him even more upset. This was his reputation. Everyone knew who Charlie Wolf was and everyone knew his job. Everyone knew all about him. Now he, Charlie

Wolf, just got fired? Worse yet, he had lost a friend, and he had acted unprofessional toward Mr. Safino.

Haunting memories came back to him of his date the other night.

The devilish Diane made a mockery of him in front of the whole restaurant. *"Oh, and who's the adolescent?"…"If you wouldn't play around with so many women, all your problems would be fixed!"*

All those eyes staring at him. His date. *"I thought you were someone different"*

*"Just take it like a man…Charlie, I'm sorry."*

*"You might as well make the best of it."*

He felt so immature, so small. He knew everyone was laughing at him. Even those who did not show it were laughing inwardly. His admiring son would now hate him, his job was just taken away, everyone would know about this. His job was his security. His life. He had no one to turn to, no one to talk about his problems with, no one to calm him down. He had no one. He drove over a straight road with a speed limit of forty-five. He was going seventy. A white Ford Explorer was coming toward him. The terrain on both sides of the road was barren flat ground. He sped up even faster as the Ford Explorer came closer. He gripped the steering wheel tightly as he traveled faster and faster while clenching his teeth in anger. Charlie let go of the steering wheel with one hand to scratch his lower leg. He veered slightly to the left. The Explorer tried to yank to the right to avoid him, but it was too late. The cars collided. Then all was a blank.

# CHAPTER 6

Charlie awakened to a room flooded with bright white light and the beeping noises of a monitor. As his vision grew sharper and clearer, he was certain he was looking up at a white ceiling. With a sore cramped back, he attempted to sit up. However, as he tried, he winced as a sharp pain struck his back, forcing him to fall back onto the bed.

All Charlie could remember was driving back home, and now he was in this unfamiliar bed. He managed to look down and seeing the sling on his arm and feeling a weight on his forehead, he took his hand and felt a bandage wrapped around his head.

The door to the room opened and a young male doctor entered wearing white doctor's scrubs. Charlie looked at him as the doctor made eye contact, "Oh Mr. Wolf, you're awake." With all the tubes attached to Charlie and the electric equipment all around him, the doctor explained,

"You were in a bad wreck. Your car is totaled, but the important thing is you're okay."

Charlie's eyes were puffy and dark circles were evident. His face was scruffy with tiny stubbles of beard. He spoke through the pain and grogginess, "What happened?"

The young doctor looked at him and then replied, "I would rather Dr. Humming tell you."

Charlie kept looking at him as the doctor turned back to his clipboard jotting down information on it. When he was finished, he flipped the pages back, folded the clipboard in his arm, and looked at Charlie brightly, "Well it looks like you're doing okay. Your pulse is normal, your breathing is normal, you were unconscious for a few hours, but your brain is functioning perfectly now. There were a few pieces of glass we had to remove, there's kind of a nasty bruise on your forehead, you sprained your right ankle, your right arm is broken, but it should heal and you should be out of that cast in a couple of months. And that's about it. Now I'm going to step out of the room and Dr. Hemming is going to come see you in a moment. Okay?"

Without ever changing the expression on his face, Charlie slowly nodded. The doctor left the room, and it was only a few seconds before another doctor came in. But this doctor was older and dressed in slacks and a tie. He shut the door behind him, pulled a chair up beside

Charlie's bed, and sat down with a smile. His eyes twinkled as he spoke, "Hello Charlie. I'm Dr. Humming. Nice to meet you." His expression and voice changed to a more serious tone, "Charlie, tell me everything you remember before you awoke here in the hospital."

This all seemed like a nightmare to Charlie and he could not think clearly or rationally. He did not know what was going on and he was not even sure how to answer the question. Finally, after Dr. Humming waited patiently for his answer, Charlie answered slowly and feebly like an old man, "Well, Dr. Humming, I'm not really sure." He smiled at his own pathetic response.

Dr. Humming clarified, "You don't remember anything at all?"

Charlie was still quite weak, but his curiosity was getting the better of him. He asked, "Doctor, could you please tell me what happened? All I really remember is driving back home from work."

As if Dr. Humming could not wait to say this, he responded, "You were traveling approximately seventy miles per hour in a forty-five mile per hour speed zone. Apparently, you swerved into the path of a white Ford Explorer traveling toward you at about forty miles per hour. You collided."

Charlie's eyes widened, "Are the other people okay?"

Dr. Humming nodded, "Yes, he's okay. It was only the driver, and he has a few minor injuries like you have, but sadly, when you hit him, his engine caught fire and he is now suffering severe third degree burns on his arm. He will be using a wheelchair for a while, but we expect him to progress to a walking aid like a cane. He will probably require an aid for the rest of his life." He paused, "Do you mind telling me now how you swerved into his car?"

Everything was like a dream; this could not be real. But Charlie somehow knew that this was reality. He truthfully replied, "I honestly don't know."

"Maybe this information will help jog your memory. After your wreck, I contacted your boss, Mr. Safino. Is this your boss?"

Charlie nodded.

"He said you were fired from your job right before that drive, and that you had stormed out of the office. You also made a cellular phone call to your ex-wife, Diane. Is that right?"

He nodded.

"I contacted her too and it seems that she is the last person you talked to before you wrecked. She told me that you were very upset because you were fired, and you hung up on her abruptly. Is all this true?"

"Yes."

Dr. Humming leaned in close to him, "Now Charlie, let's be honest and truthful with one another. I'm your friend. Okay?"

Charlie nodded.

"It seems like you were very upset that you lost your job right before you had your wreck. Do you think this could have possibly affected you or caused this wreck in any-way?"

Charlie could not sit up but his face became a little confused and upset and he raised his voice a little, "What are you trying to say?"

"I think you know what I'm trying to say. All this was happening, you were telling Mr. Safino that you had nothing in life, you are divorced, have a dysfunctional family, and you felt like your life was over yesterday. You were driving extremely fast. You were angry. Weren't you?"

"Yeah, pretty angry."

"Good, you're being honest. That's good," he became serious again, "Tell me, Charlie. Do you ever suffer from depression or feelings that life is meaningless?"

Charlie was too smart to fall for these questions. He became quickly aggravated, "Just tell me what you're trying to say here."

Dr. Humming started speaking fast, "What I'm trying to say here is that it's been reported that there were no other cars in sight when you collided, your tire marks on the road indicate that you suddenly jerked the steering wheel right when the other car approached. With all the background and evidence, it makes it apparent that this wreck could have very well been intentional on your part."

Charlie's eyes opened in horror, "Are you trying to say that I purposely ran into that other car?"

Dr. Humming sat back in his chair calmly, "That's what we're here to talk about."

"Who are you?"

"I'm a psychiatrist, Charlie."

※          ※          ※

Jonathan lay there on the hospital bed with his arm wrapped in white bandages. Sara sat in a chair by his bed. Her mascara had already streamed down her face and dried, revealing her tear tracks.

Sara ran her fingers across her eyes, "I must admit, Jonathan, it's a miracle that you're alive and, for the most part, okay."

Jonathan still lay flat on his bed, but he nodded.

"I mean it's a miracle that your head was barely touched. People in these kind of car wrecks die or are at least seriously injured, but you're going to be okay in a little while."

Without moving a muscle, Jonathan moved his eyes to look at his wife. Taking a breath, he said faintly, "I think we should pray right now," he lifted and slowly extended his hand to Sara, "take my hand."

Sara took his hand and held it tight sobbing, "Oh sweetie."

Clenching her hand, Jonathan closed his eyes, "Our Heavenly Father, we would just like to come to you right now humbled. For whatever reason, I am here in this bed right now bandaged from head to toe. I do not know what your divine plan is right now, but thank you, thank you for letting me live on earth right now. I just ask that you will take this experience and turn me into a more Godly man. In Your Son, Jesus' name I pray. Amen."

Sara repeated, "Amen."

Dr. Humming stood in the doorway with a hand on the door, "I hope I'm not interrupting anything."

"Oh, no. Come in," said Jonathan pleasantly.

Dr. Humming came in and closed the door behind him. He pulled up another chair and sat next to Sara. He looked at both of them as he spoke, "I just spoke to the man who was involved in the collision. He has no recollection of anything. We have reason to believe that it was possibly a suicide attempt, but we are not sure yet. He doesn't have any burns on him, but he does have broken bones. But I can assure you both that he will be under specialized care."

Sara spoke a little flustered, "Well I just want to be sure that that he is treated justly."

Jonathan soothed her, "Sara, it's okay. That's not important right now."

Dr. Humming added in comfort, "I'm sure he will be ma'am. There's nothing to be concerned about."

"What's his name?" asked Jonathan.

Dr. Humming looked at him, "Uh, Charlie Wolf."

The name immediately struck Jonathan's memory. Charlie Wolf. His eyes widened in shock as he said anxiously, "Charlie Wolf? Oh my goodness, he was a close friend of mine when I was young." He turned to Sara, "Do you remember Charlie?"

Sara's worn out face tensed as she thought, "It sounds familiar."

Jonathan's body was filled with energy again. He turned to Dr. Humming with the astonished look on his face, "I know him. I'm sure if you mention my name to him, he would remember me too." He turned his head to the wall. What am I going to do? Well, before Jonathan could decide what to do about Charlie, he had to be certain of every detail.

He turned back to Dr. Humming, "Just find out what his intentions were."

❦          ❦          ❦

The door opened and Charlie had to lift his head to see who was coming in. He was still lying flat on his bed. He was more alert now, but every limb in his body was still sore. Diane appeared in the room; her face revealed that she was upset and maybe perturbed. She stood next to his bed, leaned on the wall, and folded her arms, "Could you just be honest with me?"

Charlie nodded, "Sure."

Diane let out a heavy sigh and asked, "Well first of all: are you okay?"

"Splendid."

"Alright good. Was this really suicidal, Charlie?"

Charlie blew through his lips and then replied, "No, of course not. And as a matter of fact, I am really offended and scared that I'm actually being accused of that."

Diane put her hand over her heart and let out a sigh in semi-relief, "Okay, I hope you're telling the truth. But seriously, if this was suicidal, Dr. Humming can help you with that. Do you know who you hit by the way?"

"Who?"

"Your old friend, Jonathan Mitchell."

"I hit Jonathan Mitchell?" he said stunned.

Diane nodded looking at the floor, "Yeah."

"I can't believe that." He changed the subject, "Diane, listen to me. I am not suicidal. I was having a bad day that day and that *did* make me drive a little fast, but I did *not* intentionally drive my car into another car. I did not want to die, and I did not want to kill anyone. I swear. Do you understand? Please, you have to help me."

Diane did not know what to think, "Charlie, I am confused and I just don't know what to do. I guess I believe you, and I don't want you to be accused of something you didn't do."

Charlie couldn't hide a smile, "Wow, that was the nicest thing you've said in a long time."

She gave him a dirty look in reply.

"Where's Franklin?"

"He's outside," she answered.

"Can I talk to him? Alone?"

Diane nodded and left the room. Shortly after she left, Franklin came in.

Charlie motioned, "Hey Franklin. Come here."

Franklin walked up to him.

"So how are things at home?" asked Charlie.

Franklin nodded, "They're going pretty good. Dad, did you really try to kill Pastor Mitchell?"

"Is Pastor Mitchell that driver I hit?"

Franklin nodded.

Charlie was shocked to hear his own son asking him this, "Who said I tried to kill Pastor Mitchell?"

"Well that's what I heard Mom talking about."

"Your mom said that?"

"Yeah."

Charlie sighed heavily and then looked at his son straight in the eye enunciating every word he said, "Now listen to me, Franklin. You have to understand that your mother does everything in her power to always make me look like the bad guy to you. And I am telling you the truth when I say that having a wreck with that man was entirely accidental. Okay? Do you believe me?"

Franklin's eyes became moist with tears as he nodded, "I guess so."

It really hurt Charlie to see his son like this. He extended his arms and said compassionately, "Come here."

Franklin leaned into his father and wrapped his arms around his neck.

Jonathan was trapped barely conscious. A flood of heat drowned his whole body as his head laid on the scorching steering wheel. All he could make out with his vision was thick blue smoke rising in front of him. Hurried voices echoed all around him.

*"Can you hear me? Can you hear me?"*

Suddenly he felt a tug on his body as someone or some few carried him out of the vehicle. He looked down at his arm. He tried to scream at the hideousness of his arm, but his voice was muted. He continued to stare at his black arm disfigured, burned.

He looked up and saw a sloppy scruffy figure walking towards him. Rags hung around him and he had an unkempt beard. It was the homeless man who had walked into one of his church services. He continued walking towards him as Jonathan glanced around sensing danger. All the firemen and rescue workers were gone and Jonathan was alone with this stranger. He tried running away, but he was in too much pain.

The man finally stopped a few feet away from Jonathan and in a gruff rude voice, he spoke, *"Well, well, well. It looks like you've got a little scar on your arm there."*

Jonathan looked down at his arm and then looked back at the man panicked.

*"Now we're the same. Now we're brothers. Not by blood of course though,"* he grinned revealing only a few teeth and chuckled to himself, *"but you know what I mean. Right? Now you know how it feels to not be pretty. Now you know how it feels to be repulsive."*

Jonathan sat straight up in his hospital bed breathing heavily. Sweat dripped down his face and his pajamas stuck to his back. Everything was dark and silent in his hospital room. He sighed realizing that he had had a nightmare. Looking down at his bandaged arm, he whispered to himself, "What's the difference now? What's the difference now?"

He looked at the clock by his bed—10:31. After staring at the red numbers for a few seconds, Jonathan quickly grabbed the telephone and held it on front of his face. His thumb quivered over the numbers as if a force was holding him back from dialing. Finally, he dialed the number and held the phone to his ear. "Hey Dr. Humming," he spoke, "It's Jonathan."

❧          ❧          ❧

"Mr. Wolf?" a doctor opened the door.

Charlie turned his head on his pillow to look at him.

"I'm here to report to you that you are free from any criminal charges. You won't be required to see Dr. Humming anymore."

Charlie sighed in relief, "Thank God. How did this happen?"

The doctor replied, "It was all in the hands of Jonathan Mitchell."

Although he had not seen Jonathan in years, Charlie thanked him in his own mind.

# CHAPTER 7

About three months passed as Reverend Mitchell recovered from his injuries, and now he was back at the First Baptist Church.

The assistant pastor stood in the pulpit and spoke with happiness evident on his face and in his voice, "As you all know, Reverend Mitchell was in a car wreck and suffered serious injuries and burns. But after a few months, the Lord healed him, and even though he has not fully regained his strength, his spirit is stronger than ever. So please join me as we welcome Jonathan Mitchell back."

Applause resounded throughout the sanctuary as the congregation stood and clapped. Jonathan slowly stood from his chair on the platform and with a modest smile on his face, a bandage still on his arm, and resting his weight on a cane, he staggered towards the assistant pastor and used his good arm to embrace him. Then he walked up to the pulpit.

Jonathan gazed at the congregation and spoke with a voice that was not so booming and eloquent as it used to be, "Thank you for such a warm welcome back. It's so great to be home. "I'm here not to rejoice that I'm alive, but to rejoice that I had that wreck."

The people listened intently to hear his point. "I thank God every day that I am using a cane and that my arm is mutilated. I thank God for the scar I have now that reminds me that I am just a man and that God sees me as just as dirty and wretched as we see a homeless beggar. I thank God for letting me realize that being a pastor does not make me any more worthy than the scum of society. I believe things happen for a reason and while most of you think that I should be thankful for living, I'm really thankful for suffering.

"As you can see, I have no notes, no Bible verses, no traditional outline for my sermon this morning. I also do not want to fill a thirty-minute time segment. This morning I just want to express to you what being a Christian means to me. It has nothing to do with music, preaching, or church. It has to do with what God instructs us to do in the Bible.

"As Christians, we are not called to worry about the people who are not Christians and criticize the secular world. We are not called to build huge churches for money and popularity or to compete against each other and to join as many Bible studies as we can and gossip about fellow Christians who make mistakes. We are called to be examples to other people and to reflect Christ through our lives, which means to give the greatest love that anyone can give. Let us love with actions and deeds. Christianity is not another religion; it is the way to life. We need to live like Christ and give to people less fortunate, help the people who need help, and reach out to the people who need love the most.

"From now on, this church is not going to be the First Baptist club. It is going to be a light to this city. So why do Christians suffer? Part of the reason is to teach us; and, I admit, part of it we will never know. This is all I wanted to say this morning. Thank you."

Everyone applauded again. Scott sat in the front as a smile crept onto his face. This makes sense, he thought.

❋          ❋          ❋

Charlie drove a Ford sedan for the first time. He had completely recovered from his serious injuries, but he still had a bump on his forehead. Franklin sat in the passenger seat as they drove on the flat road with the afternoon sun sending rays through the tree branches on either side of the road.

Charlie took one hand off the steering wheel and shook his finger to speak, "See, Franklin, this is the problem with preachers. They immediately jump to conclusions without any proof and they go to the extreme and call you suicidal just because you caused a wreck with them. I think it has to do with fear. Conservative people fear too much and that is why they never move forward. Those kinds of people are scared of the world and they always fear the worst in every situation."

Franklin just looked at him.

"Your mom is the same way, Franklin. She fears the worst in every situation when really, if you think about it, anything could go wrong in any situation, but you can't live life in fear. Nothing would ever get done."

Franklin spoke, "Did you ever see him afterwards?"

"See who?"

"Pastor Mitchell."

"No, I never saw him."

"Why not?" asked Franklin.

Charlie thought for a second and then answered, "Well, I just didn't want to see him."

"But he was your best friend."

Charlie stammered a bit, "Yeah, but he's a pastor now and I didn't feel like hearing him say this or that."

Franklin thought for a second and then added, "So were you scared of him?"

Charlie exhaled in frustration, "No, I was not scared of him, Franklin. I just wasn't in the mood."

"Oh."

The Ford pulled into the apartment garage and Charlie and his son walked into his apartment. Charlie walked over to the kitchen and started pulling pots out of the cabinets, "Alright, it's fall, so we're going to cook some fall food: sweet potatoes, squash, chicken, and pumpkin pie. Does that sound good?"

Franklin sat down on the sofa and nodded up and down.

"Okay, good."

"Hey, dad?"

Charlie did not look up as he focused on setting the oven, "What?"

"Why can't you find a job?"

Charlie's voice rose a little, "It's not that I can't find a job. I still work. I just don't have my biggest job anymore."

Franklin asked another question, "Why don't you go to church?"

Still not looking up, Charlie explained, "I don't go to church because I'm just too busy."

"You're too busy to worship God?"

"You don't have to go to church to be a Christian. Church is a manmade place where they just make you feel guilty. You can still be a good person and not go to church. In fact, you can still be a Christian and not go to church." Charlie stopped and looked up at his son, "What did your mom tell you?"

"She just said you don't go to church, and you can't find a job."

Charlie slammed down a pot on the kitchen counter and spoke with his eyes fixed on Franklin, "You can't listen to your mom. She has no sense and she doesn't even know the big picture behind things. She's just close-minded. I'm open-minded and I'm more accepting of other people and of other things than she is."

Although Franklin was young, he learned a great deal from observing his parents' conflicting philosophies. He understood that his parents fell on opposite ends of the spectrum, "But aren't you being close-minded to church?"

Charlie did not reply to the question, but instead asked a rhetorical question himself, "Did your mother program you or something?"

# CHAPTER 8

The First Baptist Church was chaotic on Saturday. Actors and choir members stood on stage while the musicians sat in their places discussing specific musical measures. The sound technicians turned knobs in the back of the sanctuary while some were connecting wires and speakers. Murmuring filled the sanctuary as crew and cast members put finishing touches on their individual jobs.

In the middle of all the confusion, Scott stood in the middle with his sleeves rolled up, misplaced pieces of hair plastered on his forehead, directing every one of these people. He turned his attention to the actors on stage and gave orders, "Now you, Mary, you will step over to the left and watch Joseph as he takes the baby out of the cradle."

A gruff worker approached Scott carrying a wooden prop for the manger scene, "Does this look good, Scott?"

Scott glanced at the prop quickly and said, "Very nice, perfect." He pointed to Mary and Joseph, "Put it right behind them."

A woman appeared in the back of the sanctuary and shouted, "Scott, it's here."

Scott turned and bolted toward the woman in excitement as he walked hurriedly up the aisle, met her, and then followed her outside. It was nice getting some fresh air. A huge moving truck sat in the parking lot as two men rolled an enormous wrapped object out of the truck. Scott's heart was thumping as he waited to see it. When the object reached the parking lot, one of the men pulled off the paper. Scott's eyes grew wide with awe as he gazed at it.

The object was a gigantic, colorful, glass window depicting the story of Jesus in one picture. Using three-dimensional perspective, the background was a white, heavenly light. In front of that was a wall of red, demonic creatures twisted together blocking the light. In the middle of the demonic wall stood Christ nailed to the cross, which parted the wall and allowed a path to the heavenly light. In the front, the baby Christ was in the cradle with two angels holding him. On the frame of the window was scripture telling the story of the birth of Christ. The sun gleamed through the window giving an added living spiritual sense to it. The window captured everything the Christmas play was about.

Scott smiled, "It's beautiful."

The park was green and beautiful as a light breeze cooled everyone there and blew the palm branches. A handsome middle-aged man was playing catch with a tennis ball with a boy. Charlie caught the ball, "Now when you catch the ball, let your arm absorb it. And loosen up your hands, they're too tight." He threw the ball and Franklin caught it.

"Good. You need to do this more often." They continued throwing the ball back and forth until Charlie caught it and held it. His face fell as he spoke bluntly, "I think I might move."

Franklin was surprised, "Move? Where?"

Charlie took a deep breath, "I don't know. Somewhere new. Life is just getting old down here and I need a change."

"Like another state?"

Charlie nodded, "Yeah."

Franklin was not as close to his father as other boys, but the thought of him moving to another state shattered him, "But what about our weekends?"

This was not a big deal to Charlie, "I'll still see you a lot. Maybe not as much, but I'll still see you and I'll call you. I've just got to get away from—"

His cell phone rang. He grabbed the phone out of his pocket, read Diane's number on it, and put it on silent. Charlie added, "And I need to get a job to support you and your mom. Nothing is going to change."

The cell phone rang again. Rolling his eyes, Charlie put the phone to his ear, "What!"

A man's voice came on the other line, "Hello Charlie?"

"Yeah?"

"This is Jonathan Mitchell."

He had not talked to Jonathan in years. Charlie responded pretentiously, "Oh hey Jonathan. I haven't talked to you in a while."

"I know. It's good to hear your voice again. Do you want to meet for coffee on Monday morning?"

The invitation jolted Charlie as he searched for an answer, "Uh, well, sure I can."

"Okay. How about Starbucks at ten o'clock?"

"That's fine."

"Okay, I'll see you then Charlie."

"Okay, see you too. Bye."

❦        ❦        ❦

"So Mary, when you step off the donkey, walk around slowly showing a little anxiety. You're pretty scared because you're carrying God's Son." Scott stood in a red sweater and khakis at the bottom of the stage directing the last scene in the play.

Mary sang the slow, inspirational solo.

"Now you and Joseph exit the stage. Shepherds come in with candles. The music starts and the narrator begins."

The background music started on the sound system as the tall male narrator stood to the side talking about the birth of Jesus.

When he was finished, Scott pointed to the manger, "Smile at the baby…Now Joseph, slowly take the baby out."

The music started building as the choir came in. At the last loud note, Scott exclaimed, "And…now!"

Joseph held the baby high as the blue fabric background rose, revealing the glorious stained-glass window. Scott nearly leapt with joy. The music and choir were altogether as the shepherd boys raised their hands to the baby that Joseph was holding up. The best part about it was the shining window.

❦        ❦        ❦

Charlie opened the door as he stepped inside the atmospheric Starbucks. The smell of coffee met Charlie's nose and sent pleasurable signals to his brain. He wondered how one man in Seattle had such a vision for a coffee chain, building an empire out of it. Why was coffee so tempting and seductive? Why does the body crave the bitter substance?

"Charlie!" yelled a voice.

Charlie spotted Jonathan sitting at the same table as he had when he met with Scott. He still had the same light skin, combed blonde hair, and the pastoral smile on his face.

Emotionless, Charlie held up his hand as he waved and then walked towards the table. He put on a smile and shook Jonathan's hand, "Hey Jonathan. Good to see you."

"Good to see you too, Charlie."

Charlie pointed with his thumb towards the counter, "I'm going to get an espresso."

After he ordered, he sat down across from Jonathan with a paper cup of espresso.

Jonathan observed the cup and then asked, "Is that triple shot?"

Charlie nodded, "Yes it is."

"Scott got a cappuccino when I met him here. Cappuccino is milky, not as strong, more laid-back, which goes well with Scott's personality. Espresso is the strongest form of coffee you can have, and triple shot is twice as stronger than regular espresso. You must be pretty daring."

Charlie seemed uninterested as he took a sip, put the cup down, and swallowed, "You're an expert at coffee."

Jonathan laughed, "Also you didn't put any sugar or crème in your espresso, which proves my point even more."

Charlie changed the subject, "I'm sorry I never saw you after the wreck. I just never got around to it, but everything is paid for," he looked at Jonathan directly, "and I'm sorry about all this."

Jonathan simply nodded and studied him.

"I was just having a bad day," said Charlie.

Jonathan leaned against the table resting his chin on his knuckles, "Charlie, I didn't invite you here to talk about the car or wreck or anything."

Charlie noticed the cane leaning on Jonathan's chair.

"I just wanted to meet with an old friend. Don't you ever think about the past?"

Charlie hesitated and then replied truthfully, "No. I never think about the past. The past is in the past and there's nothing we can do to change it, and thinking about it doesn't help anything. I just look forward to the future. It's healthier to look forward to the future."

"Well I think so too, but it's also healthy to learn from the past. Do you see what I'm saying?"

"Do you want to know what I've learned from the past?" Charlie snapped, "I've learned that love doesn't exist, marriage doesn't work, everyone is fake, you can't trust anyone, and no one is your friend. I've also learned that the only point in life is to be successful because that is the only way to survive in the world, and the only way to be successful is to have money. So that's what I do everyday, I make money. When you don't have money and you have no one, there is no point to life. You wake up every morning and go through the same routine every day and the only way to stay happy is to not think about life but just accept it for what it is and play the games. Life is just a game we play until we die. That's what I've learned from the past." He was speaking fast, but he took a pause, "You, Jonathan, you have everything nice going for you. You have a perfect marriage, a perfect family, there are no ups and downs, you walk around happy all the time. You live in this fake world and you don't live realistically."

Jonathan asked politely, "What's unrealistic about my life?"

Charlie pointed a finger at him, "Everything goes well for you and you're a pastor so you live in your own world where God loves everyone no matter what." Charlie jammed his fingers into his own chest, "Well where has God been for me?"

"Charlie, you don't even accept God. You choose to live without Him."

Charlie already had his reply ready, "So I'm going to hell, right? I'm not a Christian, so I go to hell. Why would a good loving God send good people to hell?"

Jonathan remained calm and confident as he leaned further into Charlie and folded his arms on the table, "God does not send people to hell," he paused to let the statement sink in, "People choose hell."

"Oh, so people choose to be in eternal torture. That makes sense," Charlie said sarcastically.

"The Hebrews used many styles of writing, including metaphors. God uses metaphors in the Bible to make it easier to understand. The torment of fire is easy for anyone to grasp, so when hell is described as being a lake of fire, it is understood that no one wants to go there. Life without Christ is like permanently swimming in fire. You see, hell is a place where there is no God at all. Heaven is a place to be perfectly united with God as our heavenly Father. If people reject God's love while they're living, then they are choosing hell for themselves. If they choose life apart from God, rebelling against his commands, then they should have no room to complain about living in hell forever separated from God. Being in a place without God eternally is much worse than being in a lake of fire. That's just all we humans can comprehend."

Charlie paused as he rested his eyes on another part of the room. He had never thought about it that way before.

However, he was in a debate and he did not want to show weakness. He needed to have the last word, "So why is Jesus the only way to heaven? What's the matter with other religions like Judaism or Hinduism or Islam? They all believe in God. Why do only Christians get to go to heaven?"

"If you study other religions, they each have a totally different view of God."

"So how do you know your view of God is right?"

"Look at those other religions. It won't take long to discover glaring inconsistencies. You won't need help to find them. Then, look at the Bible. It has survived centuries without any changes, and there are no contradictions in there at all.

"For a current example, of a relatively new and fast growing religion, take a look at Mormonism. In the 1880's, Mormonism said polygamy was okay and black people could not be Mormon. Look how much has changed in that religion in the past hundred years. It had to adapt to the culture. Christianity has not ever needed to adapt to the culture and nothing has changed about the Bible since it was first written. The Bible is the Truth."

Charlie changed the subject again, "So how do you know the Bible is totally right? It was written by man and there are some errors in the Bible."

"Like what? Where are the errors?"

Charlie shifted uncomfortably, "Well…I don't know any specific examples, but there has to be some in there."

Jonathan found an example for him, "How about the seeming contradiction where one disciple says Jesus carried the cross and another disciple says someone carried the cross for him?"

"Yeah, what about that?" Charlie challenged.

"These are accounts from different people who are describing what each of them saw. It isn't difficult to imagine that Jesus carried the cross part way but because of the horrible beating he had received he was having trouble bearing the weight and so they compelled a passerby to carry it the rest of the way for him. But, is the real question, 'Who carried the cross?' The important question is, 'Did Jesus die on the cross to save Charlie?'"

Now Charlie felt as if he was losing the argument. He sat back and said, "You still can't prove to me that Jesus was the Son of God. If he's not the Son of God, how can his death on the cross help me?"

"Let me share something with you. Many people believe that Jesus was a great moral teacher, but was not the Son of God. Now tell me, how can you possibly make that argument? Like C.S. Lewis said, Jesus was a liar, a lunatic, or he really is God. If Jesus spent his whole life saying he is God, then he could not have been simply a good moral teacher. A person who calls himself the Son of

God is either lying or is psychotic—insane. A liar or a psychotic does not make for a good moral teacher."

"Then how is he God?"

"The ultimate test in determining if Jesus is the Son of God is whether the resurrection really did occur or not. Ever since Jesus died, there have been arguments against the resurrection. I know of only five that even merit discussion.

"The first argument says that the disciples stole the body out of the tomb. After the death of Jesus, all of Jesus' disciples went out to preach the Gospel. Only one died a natural death and all the rest were martyred in a painful way because they refused to stop preaching that Jesus is resurrected. This is historical record. People often lie, but the lie is meant to somehow benefit the liar. It would make no logical sense for all of the disciples to lie, because their 'lie' never benefited them.

"The second argument is that the Sanhedrin stole the body, so that the disciples couldn't steal it and claim that Jesus had been resurrected. If the Sanhedrin—people who denied that there is an afterlife—had stolen the body, they would have shown it to everyone to disprove Christianity.

"The third argument is that the women went to the wrong tomb. First of all, these women visited the tomb every day so they would not suddenly forget on the third day. Also, the women went to the disciples to report that the tomb was empty and all the disciples went to the same tomb, and there were guards. If it had been the wrong tomb, don't you think the Jewish leaders could have found the body in the right tomb? It was certainly in their best interest to do so.

"The fourth argument is mass hallucination. Hallucination just doesn't happen that way. Jesus wasn't seen on only one occasion. There are accounts of many different people seeing Jesus at different times in different places. Over five hundred people saw him at one time. The historical evidence makes it clear that if eyewitnesses can ever be trusted at any time, then the credibility of the eyewitnesses of Jesus' resurrection passes the "beyond a reasonable doubt" test over and over again. And, there were many eye witnesses. Every good lawyer would love the credibility of the eyewitness testimony given on Jesus' behalf.

"The last argument is the swoon theory. This is the theory that says that Jesus just passed out from the crucifixion. And when he was in the tomb for three days, he just woke up, having been critically injured with no food or water. Then, he moved the huge stone that had been sealed on the outside from inside the tomb—the stone that had taken at least two Roman guards to move into place. He managed to roll the stone away and sneak by the Roman guards. History is adamant about the competence of the Romans to carry out painful executions. It the Romans who were present at the cross on the day Jesus was crucified said Jesus was dead and verified his death by plunging a spear into his side so that blood and water flowed, then Jesus was dead. He was absolutely dead.

"In two thousand years, these are the best arguments scholars have come up with to disprove the resurrection. None of the arguments makes logical sense. So believing in the Resurrection does not require 'a leap of faith.'"

Intrigued but frustrated, Charlie looked at his empty cup of espresso and rotated it on the table. He finally blinked, looked up at Jonathan, shifted his weight forward, and said, "Well, it was good seeing you. I've got to go now. I have lots of stuff to do."

They both stood up as Jonathan extended his hand with a friendly smile, "It was good to talk with you, Charlie. I'll call you again sometime. Oh, and Charlie, there's going to be a production at the First Baptist Church on Christmas Eve that I would love for you to come to."

Charlie looked skeptical as he shook Jonathan's hand, "Sure, I'll think about it." With that said, he threw away his cup and walked out of Starbucks.

Charlie shut the door behind him as he walked into his apartment. He immediately walked over to the kitchen, opened one of the cabinets, and pulled out a bottle of Advil. He swallowed two pills in hopes of curing his splitting headache. Then he opened the refrigerator, pulled out a bottle of white wine, popped the top off, and poured a glass. He took the glass and sat down on his sofa exhausted. The loaded caffeine in the triple shot espresso did not help, so now he was taking the opposite approach with alcohol. Like church, Christian theology drained him. After talking with Jonathan, he did not *feel* any better about himself, only worse. Maybe Christianity was not supposed to make you feel better. Maybe it was not meant to cause a warm, fuzzy feeling.

He reached over and smacked a button on his telephone. A robotic male voice informed, *"You have ten new messages."*

The first one was Diane's voice, *"Hi Charlie—"*

Charlie pushed delete.

*"And also—"*

Delete.

*"And also—"*

Delete.

*"I can't believe you're moving. You have a son—"*
Delete.
*"Selfish, selfish, selfish!"*
Delete all.

# CHAPTER 9

It was now December. Scott ran his fingers through his hair as he sat at the table in his small house. The Christmas tree stood by a lit gas-log fire. The house was small and inexpensive, but well kept and furnished. The full moon was visible from the window next to him and the boom box on the table played a Christmas song while Scott hurriedly scribbled down notes and changes on the scattered sheets of sheet music under him. He stopped the song and played it over again working toward perfection.

Slowly, the pen stopped moving in his hand, as his brain seemed to slowly shut down. He looked up, dropped his pen, and leaned back in his chair. Placing his hands on the back of his head, he stretched his body. Christmas should not be about stressing out.

The next morning was Saturday, and Scott was back at the church working on the play. Most of the chaos was over so now he could sit back, watch the rehearsal, and then critique problems after each scene. He leaned forward as the final scene approached mouthing the words and following the action as it unfolded before him.

*Everything is dark with a dull blue light shining on the stage. Mary travels on the donkey as Joseph leads. She gets off and sings the song. Mysterious setting. The narrator speaks as Mary and Joseph step off stage. The shepherd boys come from stage left and right carrying candles. They take the animals with them. Music gets louder as Joseph and Mary appear back on stage with baby Jesus smiling at Joseph. The narrator finishes; blue light gets stronger, music louder. Joseph takes the baby and holds him up with the last note of the song. Loud, dramatic, and then backdrop rises revealing the stained-glass window.*

The music stopped as the lights went out. The scene was perfect. Scott stood up and clapped, "Good job, nicely done. That was beautiful."

"That looked marvelous," said a woman's voice speaking about the window.

Scott turned around and saw Jonathan's wife, Sara, hustling down across the pew looking perfectly made up as always. When she approached him, she smiled, "This is going to be a great production."

Scott smiled sheepishly, "Oh, thanks."

"And Jonathan just thinks—"

Scott spotted something out of the corner of his eye. He turned his head to the left and saw a young boy leaning on the stained-glass window and running his fingers across the glass. "Hey," Scott called out, "Don't touch that."

The boy apologized and walked away as Scott turned back to Sara, "Sorry, it's just really expensive."

Sara nodded and smiled, "I understand."

❧        ❧        ❧

Charlie created a romantic Christmas atmosphere in his apartment. The lights were dimmed, candles glimmered in various places, and the fire crackled in the fireplace as the flames reflected and danced on the ornaments on the pine tree. Slow jazzy Christmas music played on the stereo system as Charlie stood in front of the fireplace drinking a glass of eggnog. His face was fixed on the fire making his face glow orange. Normal people spend time with their families and loved ones on Christmas Eve, but not Charlie, he thought. He stood unmoving, his eyes glazed, until he slowly rambled over to the window that overlooked the street below.

Unusually cold for Florida that night, he saw some people strolling along the sidewalk in coats. At one specific spot to the side of the sidewalk, a man dressed up as Santa stood next to a green pot. He rang a bell as a few people walked by and dropped money in for the Salvation Army. Charlie stared at the Santa thinking about his own life. He was up in a nice apartment while this man was standing outside in the cold for hours to raise money for helpless people he didn't even know. Charlie suddenly felt a sense of warmth envelop him. He reached into his back pocket, pulled out his black wallet, shifted his eyes from the wallet to the Santa, and placing his cup of eggnog down on a table, he left his apartment to drop some money in the pot.

🍁          🍁          🍁

*Ring!* The telephone rang as Scott woke from his sleep and turned over in his bed. He reached for the telephone and put it to his ear, "Hello?"

"Scott? It's Beth." She was one of the people helping with the play.

"Yes."

She was frantic, "You're not going to believe this, but someone stole the window."

Being only half-awake, this felt like a nightmare to Scott. His blood pressure rose as he exclaimed, "What?"

"You should come over here. It's gone!"

"What time is it?" he asked frantically.

"Eight o'clock in the morning."

"I'll be right over there."

❦          ❦          ❦

After running down the hall, Scott flung open his office door. Beth, a woman in her thirties, was there. She looked up at him clearly distressed, "Should we call the police?"

Scott was still trying to catch his breath, but managed to speak, "Show me where it was."

Beth led him to the storage room where all the props were kept. The wall that the window had been leaning against was bare. Scott raised his hands to his head, "How did he take it?"

Beth swiftly walked outside the room and pointed to double doors that led to the back of the church.

"Can one person carry that thing?"

She thought for a second, "A strong person could."

Scott immediately dashed to the double doors and stopped outside. He turned his head all around to see nothing but air conditioning units and the concrete pallet where they stood. Then, feeling hopeless and helpless, he turned around to look at Beth who was standing in the doorway and stated the obvious, "The play's tonight."

She remained as calm as she could as she stated the obvious, "We should call the police."

❋             ❋             ❋

Books sat on the bookshelf against the wall and pictures decorated Jonathan's desk. Scott sat back in a chair facing Jonathan who was sitting behind his desk. Jonathan leaned in and folded his arms on his desk, "Well, Scott, the police are searching and doing the best they can to find out who did this."

"But Jonathan, why would anyone steal a stained-glass window? What are they going to do with it?"

Jonathan raised his eyebrows and changed his position in his chair, "Well I don't know. Maybe they're planning to sell it. It's very valuable. Or maybe they like the way it looks."

Scott turned his head and looked at him at an angle, "Do you find this terrible or is it just me?"

"I do think it's terrible, but the show must go on."

"But that was the best part of the show." Scott sat up and started gathering himself, "We're going to have to reschedule this."

Jonathan held out his hand with his palm downward as if he was calming down a little boy, "No, no, no Scott. Listen, the stained-glass window was a nice prop, but it didn't make the play what it is. Yes, it adds a little drama, but the message is still the same. You can't let a materialistic matter stop you from glorifying God. If you postpone the play, you are letting Satan win."

Scott bit his lower lip and nodded grudgingly, "Alright."

❄     ❄     ❄

At 6:55, most people were settling down into their pews. The lights were dimmed, it was dark outside, and the pianist played a few light Christmas melodies as more people walked in. Jonathan sat in the front pew wearing a coat and tie with his cane propped next to him against the pew. Sara sat next to Jonathan wearing a red Christmas dress talking to a woman behind her. The director, Scott Taverns, wore a coat and tie as he stood with the sound crew in the back studying everyone who walked, looking for possible suspects for the stolen window.

Scott looked at his watch. 7:00. He sat down in a chair next to the sound manager, "Alright, time to get started. Turn off the lights."

The sound manager turned a knob slowly as the sanctuary lights gradually dimmed to total darkness. That was the signal for everyone to turn around in their seats and stop talking. When the sanctuary was silent, the small band started playing as the first scene started. Scott exhaled. There was no need to think about the window anymore; it was gone and there was nothing he could do about it now.

Jonathan discreetly turned his head around to take a quick survey of the attendance. He narrowed his eyes to better view the open double doors at the back. Charlie Wolf shut the door behind him softly, trying not to be noticed. A faint smile of joy appeared on Jonathan's face as he turned around to face the front. Charlie had come.

🍁          🍁          🍁

Meanwhile, Diane and Franklin were having dinner at Diane's parents' house. The kitchen was bright and bustling with people, conversation, and laughter. Holly hung in various places throughout the cozy house as Christmas music played on the radio. All the brothers, sisters, aunts, uncles, and cousins were there preparing for a nice dinner.

Diane's mother turned to her, "Franklin tells me that Charlie's moving."

Diane smiled and let out a frustrated sigh, "Yeah, that's what he says, but he says a lot of stuff that he never does."

Her mother laughed.

🍁          🍁          🍁

The end of the performance was approaching. Scott leaned forward against the sound box with his face fixed on the stage, anticipating every movement, willing everything to run perfectly. Mary's song was over and now the narrator spoke. He said his last line as the music rose and Joseph lifted the baby in harmony with the choir and musical instruments.

Scott leaned toward the sound manager, "We need lots of light."

Bright blue and white lights beamed onto the stage while the backdrop never moved to reveal the stained-glass window. Instead, the blue background stayed. The scene was actually more powerful than he expected. The singing and music stopped and the lights went out as Scott rushed out the back door, went around to the side where no one could see him, and hustled to the stage. Applause filled the room as people stood up and cheered at the moving and inspiring production. Scott halted at the side of the stage, put on a smile, and walked up the steps onto the stage. The applause became louder as he stood on the stage with the lights on him.

He held a microphone in his right hand, and after the clapping concluded, he lifted the microphone to his mouth and spoke swiftly, "On behalf of the First Baptist Church, we thank you for coming out here tonight and we hope you all have a wonderful and glorious Christmas."

Suddenly the disposition of the audience turned to surprise and excitement as their eyes widened and many jaws dropped. They did not look at Scott anymore, but behind him. Scott turned around and there standing in its proper place was the colorful stained-glass window shining all the colors of the spectrum onto the congregation. Filled with shock, disbelief, and happiness, he turned back to face the congregation. This time, his smile was authentic as he spoke, "Merry Christmas." Then he waved, signaling they could leave.

Scott looked at the left wing of the stage. Beth, looking just as happy as Scott, mouthed an exaggerated "surprise."

He walked excitedly towards her and once he was close enough, he asked, "What happened?"

"He brought it back," she answered.

Jonathan hobbled onto the stage and approached Scott with a huge smile, his face turning red with delight. Throwing his bandaged arm into the air he exclaimed, "Praise the Lord! That was a great show, Scott. It really moved me, but thank the Lord the window is back."

Scott nodded in agreement, "Where's the guy who stole it?"

Jonathan replied, "I don't know. What happened?"

"Beth said he brought it back."

Jonathan was pleasantly surprised, "Are you kidding? That's great."

Beth stepped in, "We better go outside to discuss this. He's there right now."

"Alright." Scott looked back at the window and noticed a piece of paper taped on it towards the bottom. "I'll be right there," he said.

Jonathan, Beth, and Sara left to walk out of the sanctuary. Scott walked over to the piece of paper curiously. He ripped it off the window, unfolded it, and in scratchy handwriting it read, *"THANK U, SORRY IF I SCARED U WHEN I CAME INTO YOR CHURCH."*

Scott reread it as he pondered for a moment. Thank you for what? Who scared us when he came in? The message suddenly became clear to him. The homeless man who came in one Sunday to beg for money took the window. The man knew it was expensive. He knew we placed high value on it. He knew it was an essential part of the show and that stealing it would cause an uproar, and it did. But why did he thank us?

Jonathan immediately walked into the empty sanctuary from the left door and answered his question, "He thanked us for leading him to Jesus."

Scott was confused, "How?"

Jonathan, with his eyes full of compassion, pointed to the stained glass with his good arm, "Look at it."

Scott looked it over.

"It explains the key to life. It's more than just a pretty picture."

Scott turned around to look at Jonathan and asked, "Did you talk to him?"

Jonathan nodded slowly.

"Did you let him go?"

Jonathan nodded again.

Tears filled Scott's eyes as he sniffed. Overwhelmed with guilt for idolizing the window and caring so much about bringing the thief to justice, he knelt to his knees in humility covering his face with his hands. His body jerked with sobs.

Jonathan stepped closer to him and slowly knelt down beside his lifelong friend. He placed his hand on Scott's back and said, "It's okay. Sometimes God lets bad things happen to teach us a lesson—and to humble us. Believe me, I know." Jonathan looked in the back of the sanctuary and the only person there was Charlie Wolf standing in a long dark trench coat smiling at him. Charlie turned and walked out.

🍁          🍁          🍁

It was about midnight in Charlie's apartment. He had made a personal list of things he would do on Christmas day, and now he was down to the second to last item. Sitting on the side of his bed with the lamp on the table being the only light, he picked up the telephone and dialed a familiar number, "Hi Franklin…I changed my mind about moving. I'm going to stay here…yeah, really…I'll talk about it more with you tomorrow. Okay…Merry Christmas, son." He hung up.

Charlie took a pen and marked off that item, so now he was down to the last item on his list. It read, *"Call Scott to meet for coffee."* He knew he had to make changes in his life, and he was now prepared to start—one step at a time.

1013489

Made in the USA